Little Grey Rabbit
Goes to the Sea

Alison Uttley

pictures by Margaret Tempest

This edition published 1994 by
Diamond Books
77–85 Fulham Palace Road
Hammersmith, London W6 8JB

First published 1954
© text The Alison Uttley Literary Property Trust 1987
© illustrations The Estate of Margaret Tempest 1987
This arrangement © HarperCollins*Publishers* 1987
Cover decoration by Fiona Owen
Decorated capital by Mary Cooper

Alison Uttley's original story has been abridged for this book.

ISBN 0 261 66525 1

Printed in Italy

FOREWORD

Of course you must understand that Grey Rabbit's home had no electric light or gas, and even the candles were made from pith of rushes dipped in wax from the wild bees' nests, which Squirrel found. Water there was in plenty, but it did not come from a tap. It flowed from a spring outside, which rose up from the ground and went to a brook. Grey Rabbit cooked on a fire, but it was a wood fire, there was no coal in that part of the country. Tea did not come from India, but from a little herb known very well to country people, who once dried it and used it in their cottage homes. Bread was baked from wheat ears, ground fine, and Hare and Grey Rabbit gleaned in the cornfields to get the wheat.

The doormats were plaited rushes, like country-made mats, and cushions were stuffed with wool gathered from the hedges where sheep pushed through the thorns. As for the looking-glass, Grey Rabbit found the glass, dropped from a lady's handbag, and Mole made a frame for it. Usually the animals gazed at themselves in the still pools as so many country children have done. The country ways of Grey Rabbit were the country ways known to the author.

quirrel had a cold, Hare had a cough and Grey Rabbit had the sneezes. It was all because Hare lost the key of the house one rainy night. Grey Rabbit went to visit Mrs Hedgehog and Squirrel was left at home with Hare.

"Let's go out too, Squirrel," pleaded Hare. "There are moon-shadows and mushrooms and moldy warps all over the place. We shall get home before Grey Rabbit."

"Lock the door and take the key," said Squirrel, and they ran away together, skipping under the cloudy sky, dancing in the fairy circles.

But the rain came down and Squirrel's tail was soaked, and Hare's fur was bedraggled. They were both shivering.

When they got home Grey Rabbit was crouching on the doorstep, waiting.

"A-tishoo!" said she.

"A-tishoo!" replied Hare and Squirrel.

"I think I've got a cold," said Grey Rabbit. "A-tishoo!"

"I've got a cold," said Squirrel, hastily. "A-tishoo!"

"I've got two colds," boasted Hare. "A-tishoo! A-tishoo!"

"Where's the key?" asked Grey Rabbit.

Hare felt in his pockets, he looked under a stone, under the doormat, but there was nothing. They all hunted in the pouring rain, and at last Grey Rabbit found the little key by the garden gate.

Grey Rabbit made gruel before they went to bed, but next morning they all had sore throats and bad colds.

"My missus will look after you," said Milkman Hedgehog when Grey Rabbit sneezed on the doorstep.

So they all stayed in bed and Mrs Hedgehog came to nurse the family. They drank coltsfoot tea and their throats were bandaged with soft leaves. They sucked butterscotch and sipped blackcurrant tea.

Mrs Hedgehog bustled about, running upstairs with fresh butter mixed with honey. Little Fuzzypeg came with a bucket of soup. Mole sent a bunch of fragrant wild thyme. Water-rat brought a pot of water-lily jam, and Speckledy Hen sent three eggs.

"What they want is a change of air," muttered poor Mrs Hedgehog.

Moldy Warp agreed with her.

"Come and stay underground with me," he invited them. "You need a change of air."

"Dear Moldy Warp," said Grey Rabbit. "Your house is very nice, but we are used to sunshine."

"Change of air," advised Water-rat. "Come and live on the river with me."

"Oh no," shivered Squirrel. "Too wet."

Wise Owl flew over one night and heard the sneezes.

"What's all this a-tishooing?" he said. "Squirrel, Hare and Grey Rabbit ought to have a day at the sea.

"Too-whit! Too-whee!

The beautiful sea," hooted Wise Owl.

"What is the sea?" asked Hare the next day. "I heard Wise Owl talking about it."

Fuzzypeg knew, for he went to school.

"It's water. Lots of salt water."

"I don't like water," grumbled Hare. "I don't like salt, either."

Grey Rabbit went to ask Wise Owl about colds and sneezes.

"A day at the sea," advised Wise Owl, yawning, and he flew down to accept Grey Rabbit's gift of a lardy cake.

"Where is the sea?" asked Grey Rabbit, but Wise Owl just hooted –

> "You'll get rid of your sneezes
> When you feel the sea breezes.
> Too-whit! Too-whee!
> The beautiful sea."

Moldy Warp was more helpful.

"There's a blue caravan on the common," said he. "It belongs to a brown horse, called Duke and a gipsy-man. Duke will take you to the sea."

"But-but-who will drive?" asked Hare.

"It's easy," said Mole. "Hold the reins and sing out 'Gee-up, Duke.' He knows the way."

14

Hare wasn't sure of his driving powers, so he
ran to all his special friends to invite them to
go to the sea in a caravan. Mr and Mrs
Hedgehog accepted at once, and Fuzzypeg
clapped his paws. Water-rat said he would be
delighted, and even the Mole and the
Speckledy Hen decided to go with the party.

So everybody got ready. Squirrel
made a little tent, and Grey Rabbit
packed a hamper of food. Hare fetched
the garden spade and the little bucket

which had held Fuzzypeg's soup. Moldy Warp
put a golden guinea in his pocket for "it may
come in useful," said he.

The next morning, as soon as the sun rose
and the birds were singing their hymns, the
three little animals set off dressed in their
Sunday clothes. They locked the door and
hid the key under a stone.

"A-tishoo. A-tishoo. A-tishoo!" they
sneezed, as they ran over the fields to the
common.

The Hedgehog family waited by the caravan, with Water-rat and the Speckledy Hen and Moldy Warp.

The old horse showed them the key and they unlocked the door. While they scrambled inside, he backed between the shafts and waited. Hare clambered on Duke's back and fastened the traces, and Squirrel hung a branch of nut leaves over the horse's head to keep the flies away. Then, with Hare and Moldy Warp and Squirrel on the front seat, and the others inside, they started.

"Gee-up!" cried Hare, shaking the reins.

"You needn't bother to say that," said the horse, turning his head. "I know my way. We shall be there all in good time."

Hare was disappointed, but he huddled under the rug and was silent. Moldy Warp stared at the sky, and Squirrel's bright eyes gazed about at the fields and trees. Inside the caravan Grey Rabbit, with the Hedgehog family, Water-rat and Speckledy Hen, explored. They jumped on the bed, and looked in the mirror, and tasted the cheese on a shelf.

The caravan went through villages, past farms and cottages, down leafy lanes, in the quiet dawn. They met only a few wandering animals. There was Brush the Hedgehog, camping by the road, and a Fox who gave a side-long look at the brown horse, but he did not notice Hare, Moldy Warp and Squirrel peeping from the rug.

The old horse jogged along peacefully, until he came at last to the end of a green path at the top of the cliffs.

"Here we are," he neighed.

Hare sneezed and tumbled off his seat down to the grass.

"The sea! The glorious sea!" shouted Hare, dancing to the door of the caravan.

Grey Rabbit and the others hurried out, laughing and cheering as they saw the wide green sea with the little snowy waves, curling in the distance.

"It's like a green cornfield with rows of daisies in it," said Grey Rabbit.

"It's a windy wheat-field," cried Hare.

"Unharness me," said Duke, turning his head. "I always wait here while my master goes to the village, but there's a sandy cove below the cliffs. Enjoy yourselves until the sun goes down to bathe.

"Don't be late," he called, as they collected their belongings and ran down the narrow track to the sea. There were sea-pinks and many a flower Grey Rabbit had not seen before. Moldy Warp gathered some sea-lavender to make herb tea, and the Speckledy Hen tasted some salty worms.

When they reached the bottom (after a struggle with Mrs Hedgehog, who stuck fast in a gorse bush, and Fuzzypeg who tumbled down a crack in the rocks), they all gave little shrieks of joy. They felt the warm sand under their feet, and the strong sea air in their fur and feathers.

Mr and Mrs Hedgehog said they were too old for the sea, and rested in the shelter of the tent. The Speckledy Hen sat on a round white pebble and tried to hatch it.

"What does the sea talk about?" asked Fuzzypeg, holding tight to Grey Rabbit's hand. He was rather frightened by the little waves.

"Sea breezes. Sea breezes.

No more of your sneezes,"
whispered the sea.

Hare picked up a strand of sea-weed, but the waves came up and washed his feet. With a wild cry he ran away, but when he looked round the sea also had turned back.

"It keeps coming and going," said he.

There were several strangers on the beach. A flock of snowy seagulls walked on the sand and then swam in the water, bobbing in the waves.

A group of oyster-catchers wearing pale pink stockings played on the beach. A big black cormorant sat fishing from a rock.

"Grey Rabbit, Grey Rabbit," sang the little curling waves as they lapped at Grey Rabbit's soft little feet, and touched her grey dress. The sea-wind blew her apron like a sail, and tugged at her petticoat. It pulled Hare's red coat, and ruffled Squirrel's tail. It blew Mrs Hedgehog's prickles and nipped Mr Hedgehog's nose, and tossed Fuzzypeg's smock over his head. Then it tried to grab Water-rat's ruffles, and it fluttered Mrs Speckledy Hen's feathers, so that she had to leave her white stone egg and hide in the rocks for a time.

"Wise Owl said the sea would take our tishoos away, but I am going to sneeze," announced Grey Rabbit. Hare and Squirrel both wrinkled up their noses, as they felt a sneeze coming.

"A-tishoo! A-tishoo! A-tishoo!" they all sneezed together. They made such a noise that even the seagulls were startled and they flew away. The pretty oyster-catchers ran swiftly on their toes, and the dark cormorant dived into the sea.

The breeze caught those sneezes and tossed them up in the air. They floated away like baby clouds in the blue sky.

"My tishoo has gone," cried Grey Rabbit. "I'm quite well! Hurray!"

"Mine's gone too," added Squirrel.

"Hurray! Both my tishoos have flown away!" laughed Hare, and the three animals danced on the sand, waving their paws.

Then Grey Rabbit lifted up her grey skirt and paddled in the sea. Fuzzypeg joined her, holding tight to her apron. Water-rat took off his velvet coat and white ruffles and swam. Hare plucked up courage, took off his red coat and rushed into the sea, and out again, as he saw a wave coming.

Squirrel, with a cockle-shell tied on her head for a hat and a garland of sea-weed round her neck, began to dance on the edge of the sea, and Moldy Warp dug a tunnel and made a mole-heap.

Suddenly there was a shout from the Hedgehogs who sat in the tent, watching.

"Thief! Robber! Bandit!" they called.

A seagull flew away with Hare's red coat and a second gull took Water-rat's frills. The birds flew to a rocky part of the cliff, where they dropped their treasures by their nests, with loud squawks to their wives and babies.

"Fine bed-covers," they cried.

The group of little animals on the beach could see the red coat and white ruffles hanging far above them on the wild rocky cliff.

"Who is going to get them back?" asked Hare, dancing with rage. "Those seagulls are varmints! They are foxes! They are weasels!"

"I'll go," said Grey Rabbit.

"And I," added Squirrel.

"Then I'll go and take care of you," said Hare, gallantly.

Water-rat and Moldy Warp had to stay to look after Mr and Mrs Hedgehog, Fuzzypeg and the Speckledy Hen, who were all rather frightened of the fierce screaming gulls, who came swooping near.

So the three little animals climbed the high dangerous rocks, and Squirrel on her nimble feet was always the first. She swung up the gorse-bushes, and skipped over the cracks. Hare leapt up and down, rushing forward and then stopping in alarm. Grey Rabbit plodded silently along behind them.

Squirrel arrived first at the ledge where the seagulls' nests lay. Little grey gulls were toddling about, but when Squirrel came near the

36

mother gulls pecked fiercely at her head.
Luckily Squirrel wore the cockleshell hat she
had picked up on the beach, and this
protected her.

"Oh! Oh!" screamed the gulls. "You have a
very hard head."

"I want Hare's coat and Water-rat's frills,"
said Squirrel, trembling with fright.

Then Hare's head popped round the corner
and Grey Rabbit's startled little face
appeared.

The gulls swooped at them, but Grey Rabbit shook her apron in their faces, and Hare gave a queer shrill cry, remarkably like Wise Owl's call.

"Too-whit! Too-whee-ee-ee!

The horrible sea!" he hooted, and he threw pebbles at the birds.

The noise frightened the gulls away for a moment, and the three seized the red coat and the torn snowy frills, and ran off, tumbling, rolling, tearing their fur, as they fell down the cliff.

Hare put on his coat and brushed himself. Squirrel combed her tail. Grey Rabbit pulled thorns from her fur.

"Did you hear what I said to those gulls?" asked Hare. "I frightened them away. I pretended I was Wise Owl."

Mrs Hedgehog lighted a fire of driftwood, and they filled the kettle from a stream that ran down the rocks. Then, with the bright fire crackling, and the tea brewing, and the food spread out, they enjoyed the picnic and forgot their troubles.

"Now for a sand pie," said Hare, when all the food was eaten.

He filled his bucket with sand, and the rest watched, for Hare was sometimes very clever at doing things. He patted the top firm, and turned it upside down. Then he slowly lifted the bucket.

There was a lovely golden pie, as nice to look at as Grey Rabbit's sponge pudding!

"Oh-O-O-O," cried little Fuzzypeg, and Mrs Hedgehog opened her eyes wide in surprise.

They all had a taste, but nobody liked it very much. But Hare was so proud of his first pie he made another and another, until he had a ring of them. Squirrel put a cockleshell on each turret, Grey Rabbit draped sea-weed about them, and little Fuzzypeg found pebbles to adorn them.

Hare leapt over them, and Fuzzypeg followed, crying "Follow my leader."

They wandered along the sandy strip and found beautiful pebbles, and pearly shells. Grey Rabbit picked up a starfish and Squirrel found a mermaid's purse.

Hare found a long razor-shell, Fuzzypeg gathered a lot of sea-weed balloons, and Water-rat discovered a prickly sea-urchin.

So the happy day passed, and the sun moved down to the sea to bathe in a flood of gold.

"What time is it, Hare?" asked Grey Rabbit.

Hare looked at his watch. The fingers pointed as usual to twelve o'clock. The watch had not kept time since Hare once stirred his tea with it. He dipped the watch in the sea and listened.

"Tick Tack,

Time to go back," said the fat little watch, and the fingers began to move.

"The sea has cured my watch too," cried Hare.

They put the starfish in the bucket which they half-filled with water. They twined sea-weed round their necks, stuffed their pockets with striped pebbles, and wandered wearily up the steep track.

"Hurry," cried Duke, who was expecting them. "The sun is getting into the sea."

Hare fastened the horse's traces, and clambered inside the caravan. Everyone got into the bed, and nobody bothered to drive.

The horse jogged along the lanes, and the first stars pricked the evening sky.

Inside the caravan all was quiet, for every little animal was fast asleep.

They reached the common at midnight without any more adventures, and, yawning, they tumbled out on the grass. Grey Rabbit locked the door and Hare unharnessed the horse.

The gipsy lay under a bush wrapped in a coat, snoring, so after whispering their thanks to Duke they all hurried home.